Kimmy and her parents are moving h
closer to Kimmy's grandparents.
Kimmy is not happy about this change, which means leaving her friends and home behind.
Kimmy sulks all the way to nana and grandpa's house.
Kimmy's inquisitive nature and active imagination leads her on an exploration journey, where she discovers a new friend.

Author: Judith Samuels

ACKNOWLEDGEMENTS

This book is dedicated to my beautiful belated sister Winsome Hermitt (Cutie). My loving, patient, adorable husband Larry; creative encouraging daughters Charmaine and Nicole and my darling grandchildren Kimora and Ava-Simone. You have all inspired the creation of this book. You have brought me so much joy and remind me to enjoy each and every day. You are such amazing blessings in my life, thank you.

A very special and warm thank you to my hero Dave for rescuing this book. Huge thank you to my dear friends who have supported, reviewed and listened to me vent my frustrations. You know who you are, thank you for being there.

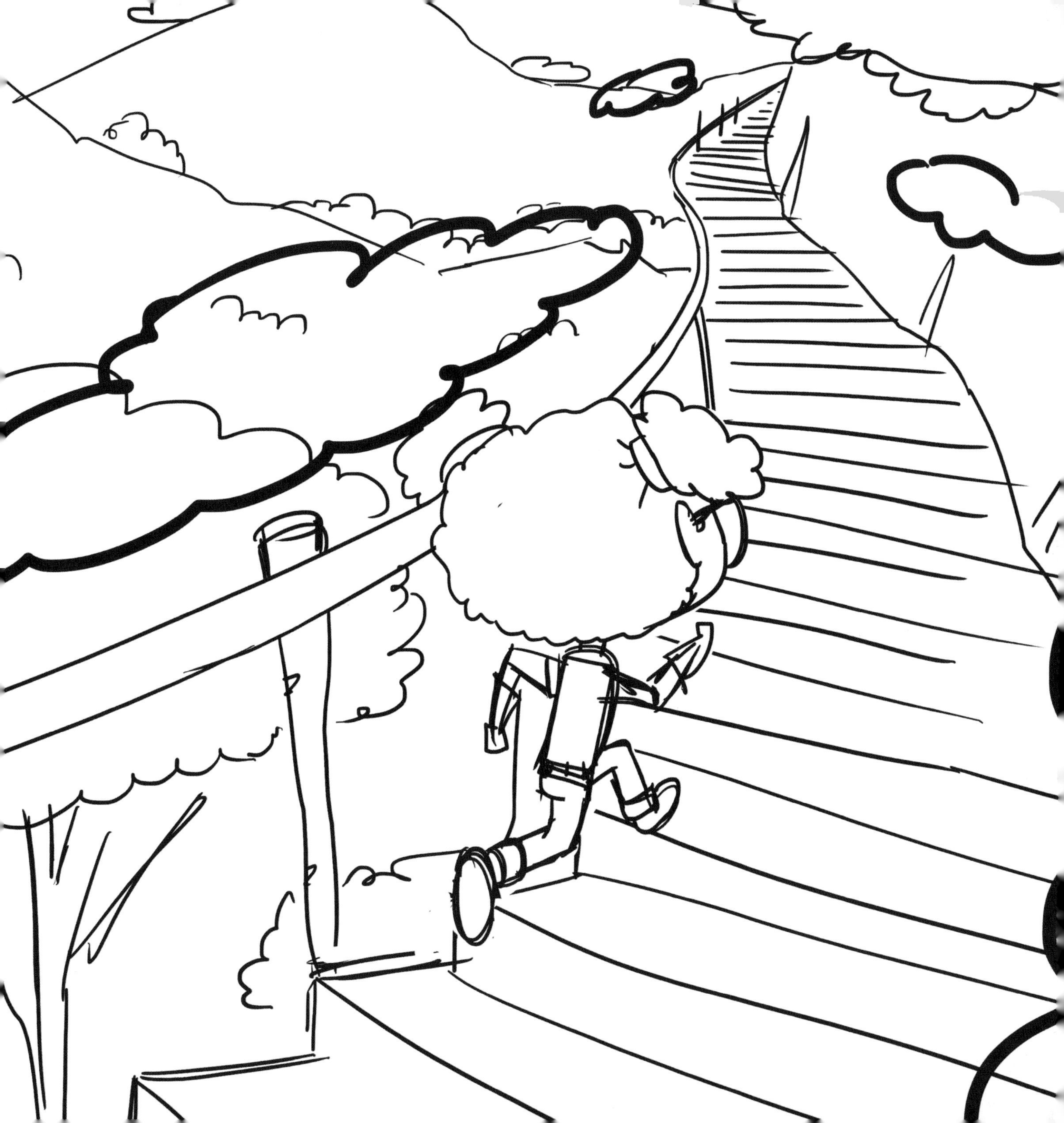

Nana Judy and Grandpa Jim were very excited. Their hearts pounded like a beating drum, Bu-boop! Bu-boop! Bu-boop!
As they awaited the arrival of their daughter Ava and her family. Nana Judy sat rocking while thinking about Kimmy when suddenly they heard the sound of a car, vroom-vroom!

Kimmy sat pouting in the car. She was four and a quarter, and this was her very first visit to Nana Judy and Grandpa Jim's, but everything looked different to the pictures she had imagined.

Kimmy watched suspiciously as her mummy hugged Nana Judy tightly. Nana Judy stretched her arms towards Kimmy asking her for a hug, but Kimmy frowned even more and shook her head stubbornly.

Kimmy wanted to go back to her old house but mummy and daddy told her that they had to live in their new house, closer to Nana Judy and Grandpa Jim. Daddy assured Kimmy she would make new friends and love their new house even more, but Kimmy felt very, very sad.

The grown-ups chatted nonstop and Kimmy got very bored. Kimmy tried to climb into Nana's rocking chair, but each time, the chair would rock forward and tilt her out. Nana Judy smiled as she scooped up Kimmy and gently placed her onto the rocking chair.

Kimmy closed her eyes and rocked... and rocked... and rocked. In her imagination, she was on a pirate ship being rocked by huge waves... Splash! Splash! Splash! She was the best pirate to ever sail the seas!

Next, Kimmy was a huge jelly being wobbled back and forth as she was taken to a giant tea party... wibble, wobble, wibble, wobble! Then... she was a cowgirl being rocked back and forth by the movement of her horse... hehaawwww!

"What on earth are you doing Kimmy?" her mummy asked. Kimmy opened her eyes and her mummy was standing in front of her frowning. "I'm using my imagination!" Kimmy said excitedly. "Can't you use your imagination more quietly?" mummy asked. Kimmy climbed off the chair and wandered off.

Kimmy's eyes lit up when she saw the stairs, and she imagined it was Mount Everest. She began to climb her imaginary mountain, dodging giant snowballs .. woosh. Just as she reached the top of the mountain she heard a noise... tap, tap, tap, tap, tap! "What is that?" Kimmy whispered.

Kimmy followed the tapping sound into a bedroom and discovered the noise was coming from a tall wardrobe. Kimmy gently opened the door but could not see anything out of the ordinary. But she could still hear, tap, tap, tap!

Kimmy was curious. What could be making the noise inside? Could it be a monster? But it would have to be a small monster. Maybe it could be a spider with a drum? But it would have to be a big spider to play the drum. Then... tap, tap, tap!

Kimmy jumped up and down, leaping like a ballerina but she could not see what was on the top shelf. Kimmy then climbed onto the bed and tried to jump even higher to see what was making that noise, but still could not see what or who was making the tap, tap, tap sound.

Kimmy dragged a chair across the room and climbed onto it. She tipped on her toes, but the shelf was too high. Kimmy stretched her arms and tipped and tipped until the chair began to wobble. She swiftly grabbed the back of the chair to stop herself from falling. "Phew!" she mumbled.

Kimmy decided to feel around with her hands, so she reached up again, hoping that it wasn't a small monster or a spider and that if it was, it wouldn't be the kind of monster or spider who eats little girls' fingers.

Kimmy reached up and stretched as far as she could, and the chair wobbled a little bit. Kimmy continued to stretch up on to the very tip of her toes, and the chair wobbled and wobbled, then... tap, tap, tap... CRASH!

Kimmy, the chair, and the wardrobe had fallen, but Kimmy didn't cry. Kimmy's eyes were widened as she stared at a slightly rusty, dusty, pink and yellow tin that tapped, tapped and tapped.

Mummy, Daddy, Grandpa Jim and Nana Judy, rushed up the stairs. "Kimmy! Kimmy!" mummy shouted. "Are you ok?" "I'm alright mummy," Kimmy said softly. Daddy and Grandpa lifted the wardrobe and were surprised to find Kimmy sitting on the floor with a big grin on her face hugging Tin Dolly!

Tin Dolly's heart leapt with joy. She was so happy to be out of her tin because it was dark and lonely in there. Tin Dolly now had someone to love and share her new adventures with.

To Kimmy, Tin Dolly felt soft, warm and comforting.

Kimmy noticed the ruby ring on Tin Dolly's finger as it shimmered brightly. Lifting Tin Dolly's hand Kimmy exclaimed, "So this is what you used to make the tapping sound!" Kimmy had no idea about the magical adventures she was going to experience with Tin Dolly!

Thank you for joining Kimmy on her journey of discovery. Keep a look out for our next adventure.

Kimmy and Tin Dolly

Printed in Great Britain
by Amazon